Zelda and Ivy
THE Big PicTURE

Zelda and Ivy
THE BIG PICTURE

LAURA McGEE KVASNOSKY

CANDLEWICK PRESS

To Jake and Maxx and Benn
as they learn to read

Copyright © 2010 by Laura McGee Kvasnosky

First paperback edition 2011

Library of Congress Cataloging-in-Publication Data is available.

Library of Congress Catalog Card Number 2010007545

ISBN 978-0-7636-4180-1 (hardcover)
ISBN 978-0-7636-5645-4 (paperback)

16 15 14 13 12 11
SCP 10 9 8 7 6 5 4 3 2 1

Printed in Humen, Dongguan, China

This book was typeset in Galliard and hand-lettered by the author-illustrator. The illustrations were done in gouache resist.

Candlewick Press
99 Dover Street
Somerville, Massachusetts 02144

visit us at www.candlewick.com

CONTENTS

Chapter One

MOVIE TIMES

The closer they got to the movie theater, the more Ivy worried.

"What if it's too scary?" she said. "It could give me nightmares."

"Relax," said her big sister, Zelda.

"It will be exciting," said Eugene, who lived next door and had been invited along.

"Exciting is okay," said Ivy. "But I don't like scary."

"If you ask me, the scarier, the better," said Zelda. "It's not real, it's just a movie."

Ivy worried more. "What if a bad guy

jumps out when we're not expecting it?

My heart could stop."

"Don't be silly," said Zelda. "It's just
a movie."

Ivy sat down and started munching
popcorn. Soon the theater went dark. As
the movie started, Ivy gripped the arms of
her seat.

But then she found herself caught up in the movie.

The secret agent raced after the bad guys to keep them from blowing up the city.

Ivy and Eugene leaned forward.

But Zelda ducked down behind the seat in front of her.

"What are you doing down there?" whispered Eugene.

"I think I dropped something," Zelda whispered back.

The movie got louder and scarier. The secret agent chased the bad guys through stormy seas.

Eugene and Ivy sat on the edges of their seats. Zelda was still down between the rows. They heard her chant, "It's just a movie, it's just a movie."

Up on the screen, the secret agent captured the bad guys and forced them to give up the bomb. He saved the city.

Music swelled and the lights came back on in the theater.

Zelda popped up.

"That wasn't so scary," she said.

Ivy nodded. "Not as scary as I expected. That's for sure."

Eugene grinned. "It was super! Let's buy more popcorn and see it again."

"Sounds good to me," said Ivy.

"Not me," said Zelda. She fished the last piece of popcorn out of her bag. "It wasn't scary enough."

Chapter Two

Secret Agents

One sunny day, Zelda and Ivy met Eugene on their way home from the library.

"Let's be secret agents and spy on people," said Zelda.

"Okay," said Eugene.

"First we need secret agent names," said Zelda. "I'll be Yolanda."

"Okay, Yolanda," said Ivy. "I'll be Boleo Rose."

"I'll be Steve," said Eugene. He stopped by Mrs. Brownlie's hedge and got out his notebook and a pencil.

He wrote:

Zelda = Yolanda

Ivy = Boleo Rose

I = Steve

"Glad you're taking notes, Steve," said Zelda. "Now let's choose a code word in case we have to call off the mission."

"Okay," said Eugene. "How about *halibut?*"

"Halibut," echoed Ivy. "I hope I can remember all this."

Eugene wrote:

Code word=halibut

Just then, Mrs. Brownlie came around

the corner of her house with a lawn mower.

Zelda yanked Ivy and Eugene down
behind the hedge.

"Mission One," she whispered. "Boleo
Rose, does Mrs. B. look suspicious?"

Ivy peeked through the hedge and inspected Mrs. Brownlie. "Yes," she said. "It's the goggles."

Eugene wrote:

Mission One
Mrs. B.- Why
the goggles?

"Yolanda," Ivy reported, "I think Mrs. B. is going to mow the lawn."

"Good hypothesis, Agent Boleo

Rose," said Zelda. "Let's see if that's

all she does."

Mrs. Brownlie pushed the lawn mower across the lawn toward the hedge, then stopped.

Zelda and Eugene each held their breath. Ivy giggled.

Mrs. Brownlie looked over the hedge.

"Hello there, Zelda—and Ivy and Eugene, too."

The three secret agents stood up.

"I'm Yolanda now," said Zelda. "We changed our names for reasons that must remain secret."

"Oh?" said Mrs. Brownlie.

"This is Steve and Boleo Rose."

"I see," said Mrs. Brownlie. "Nice to meet you, Yolanda and Steve and Boleo Rose." She put the lawn mower aside. "Would you like some lemonade and a little snack?"

Eugene shoved his notebook into his pocket. "Halibut," he said.

"Halibut," Zelda echoed.

"Hmm," said Mrs. Brownlie. "I'm afraid I can't offer you halibut, but I did just bake some chocolate chip cookies."

The secret agents and Mrs. Brownlie
were munching cookies when she realized
she was still wearing goggles.

"My goodness," she said. "I put these on to protect my eyes when I was mowing, and I forgot to take them off."

Zelda raised her eyebrows at Ivy and Eugene. They nodded back.

Later, when Mrs. Brownlie went into the kitchen for more cookies, Eugene took out his notebook and opened it to the Mission One page. He wrote:

Chapter Three

PLAN B

Zelda and Ivy and Eugene spent most of the day getting ready for a campout.

But just before dinner, it started to rain.

"Rats," said Eugene. "We'll have to cancel our campout."

"No way," said Zelda. "Just like a good secret agent, a good planner always has a backup plan. Here is mine. We're going to camp IN."

"Camp in?"
echoed Eugene.
"But what about
the s'mores?"

"Don't worry,"
said Zelda. "It's in
the plan."

"And what about
stars?" asked Ivy.
"I will miss counting
the falling stars."

"Trust the plan," said Zelda. She ran to her desk for a sheet of sticky-back stars and stuck them on the ceiling.

"Voilà!" she said. "The galaxies!"

Ivy still wasn't sure she liked camping in. The living room smelled like furniture polish, not grass and trees. But she helped set up the sleeping bags.

The three campers ate dinner from a cooler. Then Zelda and Ivy's mother lit a fire in the fireplace.

"That'll work," said Eugene.

They sang camp songs and roasted marshmallows.

Eugene smiled at Zelda. "Good plan!" he said, and stuffed another s'more into his mouth.

But Ivy sighed. She could hear her dad practicing his oboe in the basement. She had hoped for the rustle of wind in the trees.

Still, when it came time to go to sleep,
she snuggled into her sleeping bag just like
Zelda and Eugene. But she didn't go right
to sleep.

Ivy shined her flashlight at the sticky-back stars and listened to the rain pound the roof. The stars glinted back. If she squinted, they almost looked real.

Then one star came unglued and floated

down onto her sleeping bag. Ivy smiled.

"Look, Zelda," she said. "A falling star."

Zelda grinned back. "Just as I planned."